LITTLE MONK AND THE TIGER

"Suar, Suar—Tiger, Tiger!" The dreaded word rang through the village of Nan. The tiger with the crooked paw was raiding once more. In desperation, the silver merchant offered the choice of anything in his shop to whoever could rid the village of Mrs. Crooked forever.

All the villagers yearned for a particular shining prize. Many tried to outwit the crafty, ferocious tiger. But it was a gentle little monk—who was forbidden to harm an animal or to own silver—who won the prize and made a wise choice.

Striking full-color illustrations contrasted with handsome black-and-white drawings enhance the beauty of this tale of Thailand.

COWARD-MCCANN INC.   NEW YORK

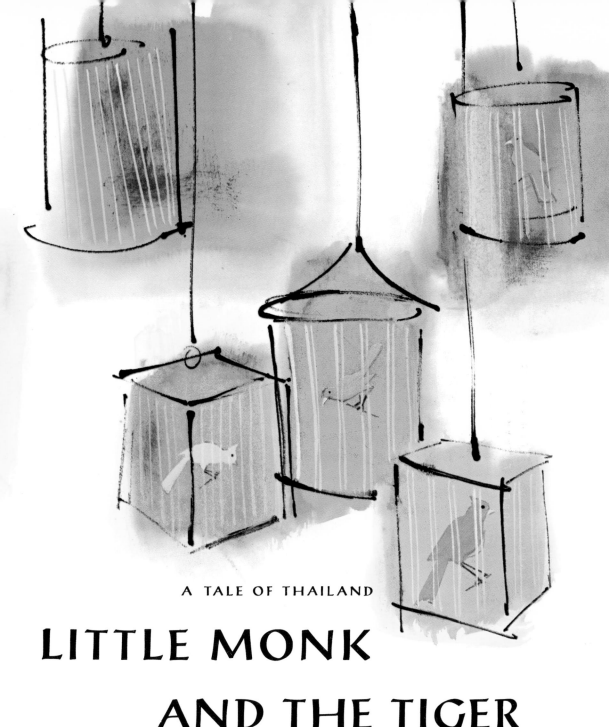

A TALE OF THAILAND

LITTLE MONK
AND THE TIGER

BY ARNOLD DOBRIN

"Suar, suar — tiger, tiger!" The call rang through the village. A boy shouted, "The tiger has carried off another fine young pig." The people in the village of Nan gathered in the square and wrung their hands.

"It is Mrs. Crooked again," one of the villagers shouted angrily. For many weeks Mrs. Crooked had raided the village of Nan. At night the villagers would hear a squeal or whimper and when they looked in the morning, a young calf or plump pig would be gone. They called the tiger that stole their animals Mrs. Crooked because one of her paws turned crookedly in.

The silver merchant, whose pig had been carried off, was very angry. "Whoever rids the village of Mrs. Crooked shall have whatever he wishes from my silver shop," he told the villagers. Everyone gathered around to admire the precious, gleaming silver objects that shone so brightly. They began to chatter so much that a sad little bird — who never sang at all — hopped from one side of his cage to the other, frightened by the noise.

A young basketmaker admired a wonderful sharp knife with a silver handle. How he could swagger through the village if he were able to thrust such a knife into his belt!

An old moneylender, who was the richest man in the village, yearned for the heavy silver bracelets that were locked away in a special glass case. How he would love to add them to his bulging trunks of gold and silver!

A boy who danced in the temple looked longingly at the shining silver crown that shone with a thousand tiny pieces of silver. He imagined how handsome he would look in the crown as he danced.

Everyone talked about what he would choose if he were to rid the village of Mrs. Crooked. But the monks who stood listening did not talk about what they wanted because everyone knows that a monk is allowed to own only three things: the bowl he begs his food with, the sandals on his feet, and the umbrella that keeps the hot sun off his head when he goes about the village.

But one monk—everyone called him Little Monk because he was the smallest of all the monks — knew that he would ask for one special thing. That is, if he were to catch Mrs. Crooked. And that was very unlikely, for monks are not permitted to harm even a small ant.

Sometimes children who were visiting from foreign countries would ask the monks, "What is a monk? What does a monk do?"

Then Little Monk would step forward and tell them, "All the boys of Thailand become monks—sometimes for only one week.

It is the believing of the people that boys will make better men and better fathers if they are monks at some time in their lives. And it is the believing of the people that they should know more about true freedom and the ways to freedom."

The next day, the young dancer went into the jungle. First he cut down some big trees and stripped them of their leaves. He drove the trunks deep into the ground and lashed them together with strips of cane. Then he made a sliding door that would slam shut as soon as a tiger entered the cage.

He put a plump young pig inside as bait, and went back to wait in the village. He waited and waited, but in the morning when he went to look, there was no tiger in the cage. Mrs. Crooked was too smart to fall into such an ordinary tiger trap.

The following day the young basketmaker went into the jungle to try his luck. He chopped down even bigger trees. He stripped them of their leaves and tied them together. Then he drove heavy spikes into them and leaned the logs against a tree like a slanted roof. He tied a young goat underneath as bait.

The basketmaker went back to the village. He could hardly wait until morning came, but when he went to the trap—just as the sun was rising over the jungle—he saw that it was still empty. Mrs. Crooked was too smart for even his clever tiger trap.

"Now I shall catch Mrs. Crooked," the shrewd money-lender said. He hired some elephants. He hired the most famous tiger hunters in Asia.

Early the next morning, before the sun rose, the men and elephants thrashed through the jungle trying to scare Mrs. Crooked out into the open. They banged and clanked on metal pots to frighten her. They thrashed and stomped. All morning they searched for Mrs. Crooked but when noontime came she still hadn't been found.

Mrs. Crooked had seen the dancer make his trap. She had seen the basketmaker make his cruel trap. And long before the money-lender and his elephants had stomped into the jungle, she had smelled the smell of man.

She had gone off to the highlands to wait until they had finished. When they grew hungry and weary, in the heat of the day, she made her way back to the village.

That day Little Monk was begging his lunch from a small
house on the very edge of the village. A kind woman filled his
bowl with rice and topped it with bright hot curry. Little Monk
began to make his way back to the temple.

As he crossed a field close to the edge of the jungle, he heard a soft whimper. Little Monk walked into the jungle and heard the whimper again. A little animal is crying, he thought and he walked farther and farther until, suddenly, he saw something move.

There, in the bamboo thicket, was a partly broken old tiger trap. And there in the grass, whimpering softly, was a tiger cub. Its paw was caught but otherwise its furry little body looked unhurt. As Little Monk bent down to pat the cub's ears he knew why Mrs. Crooked had stayed near the village of Nan. She couldn't move to another part of the jungle where food was more plentiful because she couldn't take her cub with her. Mrs. Crooked was a very good mother.

Suddenly there was a roar and a snarl and something leapt into the bamboo thicket. Mrs. Crooked was back! Ro-ar! Ro-ar! In the sunlight Little Monk saw the tiger's teeth gleaming white and strong. He saw her sharp claws ready to pounce.

But Little Monk was not afraid. He knew that Mrs. Crooked only wanted to protect her cub. Gently he lifted the rusty trap from its paw while Mrs. Crooked watched his every move. Then the cub limped over to his mother and as she gently licked him she forgot all about Little Monk.

Not far away lay the road to the city. The silver merchant, returning with his heavy boxes, saw something bright move in the jungle. It was a monk's robe and the merchant called out, "Ay, what goes on there? What monk ventures alone into a jungle full of tigers?"

Little Monk made his way back to the road. When he told what had happened, the merchant's eyes opened wide.

As soon as they arrived at the village the silver merchant excitedly called out, "People of Nan! Listen! Little Monk has freed us from Mrs. Crooked because he has found out why Mrs. Crooked wouldn't leave our poor village alone.

"Her cub was caught in one of our old tiger traps. And Mrs. Crooked is a very loving mother and certainly wouldn't leave her cub to go where food is plentiful. She preferred to fatten him with my plump pigs!" And he burst out laughing.

The villagers broke into a murmur of surprise and wonder. All the people of Nan gathered around Little Monk. The silver merchant said, "Now, Little Monk must have his reward. Anything in my silver shop!"

"No, no," the people cried. "Monks cannot own silver." And one of the monks said, "Everybody knows that a monk can own only his begging bowl, his sandals, and his umbrella."

"True, true," shouted the villagers.

"But what am I to do?" pleaded the merchant. "All the good people of Nan, here on earth — and Buddha in heaven — have heard me swear that I shall give a prize of silver to whoever rids our village of Mrs. Crooked."

Suddenly Little Monk stepped forward. "I shall accept a prize from you, good merchant. And I know exactly what I want."

As Little Monk went into the silver shop, all the villagers stood silently, their mouths gaping with curiosity and their eyes wide with wonder at the monk who would take silver.

Little Monk was in the silver shop only a few minutes. When he returned he carried a silver cage that held a small, quiet bird. "This beautiful silver cage shall go to the temple to adorn the altar on which Buddha rests." Then Little Monk opened the door of the cage and the bird flew out. "Fly free in the sky," called Little Monk. "Birds and tiger cubs were meant to live in freedom."

At the very moment the bird left the cage, Mrs. Crooked and her cub were already going deeper and deeper into the jungle. And never again did they return to the village of Nan.